# SOFTER THAN *Stone*

## BECCA SEYMOUR

Even stone
can soften…
in the right
hands.

# SOFTER THAN Stone

## BECCA SEYMOUR

RAINBOW TREE PUBLISHING

*Softer Than Stone* © 2025 by Becca Seymour

All rights reserved. No part of this book may be used or reproduced in any written, electronic, recorded, or photocopied format without the express permission from the author or publisher as allowed under the terms and conditions with which it was purchased or as strictly permitted by applicable copyright law. Any unauthorized distribution, circulation or use of this text may be a direct infringement of the author's rights, and those responsible may be liable in law accordingly. Thank you for respecting the work of this author.

*Softer Than Stone* is a work of fiction. All names, characters, events and places found therein are either from the author's imagination or used fictitiously. Any similarity to persons alive or dead, actual events, locations, or organizations is entirely coincidental and not intended by the author.

For information, contact the author: hello@beccaseymour.com

Editing: Hot Tree Editing

Cover Designer: BookSmith Design

Publisher: Rainbow Tree Publishing

Limited Edition Paperback ISBN: 978-1-923252-73-8

Original Paperback ISBN: 978-1-923252-42-4

Ebook ISBN: 978-1-923252-43-1

*For my readers,*
*This one's for you.*
*xoxo*

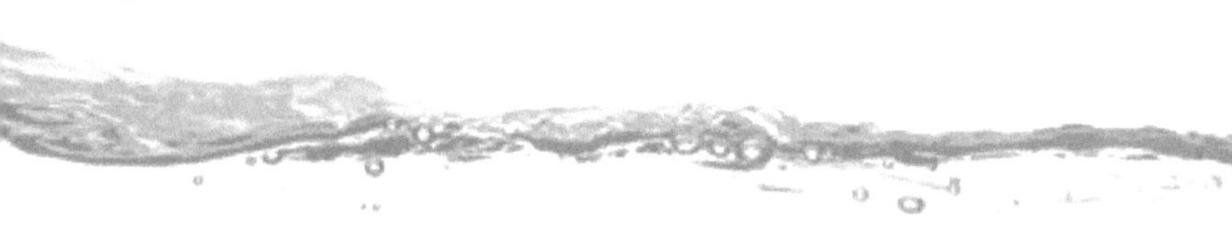

# I

## CHRIS

There was a twitch this time. Barely there. Not even countable as a fraction likely, but it was there all the same. If I'd blinked, I would have missed it. But I hadn't.

Was the fact that I was staring intently, refusing to even bat an eyelash to stop my straining eyeballs, a little intense? Most likely, but I had zero fucks to give. And whatever was less than zero when it meant I'd caught the barest of lip twitches from Waru.

Fuck, he was beautiful.

Handsome when he scowled. Striking when he cussed and threw out orders. And hands-down mesmerising when he smiled. Though was it technically a smile if the quirk of just one side of his mouth only made it up? Truth was, it didn't matter.

What should have mattered was me doing a better job of observing the restaurant floor and getting ready to intercept my mark after her meeting. All of that seemed impossible—and would likely get me a major arse-kicking from my boss, Lucas. In fairness, though, practically every one of my colleagues, boss man included, had been more than a little distracted by a sweet arse and a sexy smile while being on the job.

Except for Kent maybe.

The only thing she tended to be distracted by was whose balls she could bust. It was an art form, and hell if she didn't have an impressive knack for it.

But back to Waru, who I absolutely should not be dreaming of gobbling up and laying across the stainless steel countertop he usually stood next to as he checked the meals before the waitstaff ran them out to customers. But here I was.

Fortunately, none of the customers could see me drooling. Nor could they see how hypnotic Waru became when a pissed-off, reached-the-end-of-his-tether expression turned his brown cheeks ruddy. They couldn't see the way he gnawed at his poor lip, either, to the point I scented blood a time or two. Fuck, he all but lit up. All pouty and growly, his panther seemed to be just below the surface.

I wondered just how much one of his kitchen staff would have to screw up to bring even more out. Not that I should want to see that happen in real time—especially in his crowded restaurant—but damn if the thought of shifting into my lion form and rubbing along his sleek black fur didn't get me hard.

"Copy, Chris. Over."

I clicked the mic on my discreet earpiece, responding immediately to Smythe, who was my tech support on this mission. "Copy. All quiet. Over."

Another scan of the restaurant from the two-way mirror off the side of the kitchen showed no sign of my mark. I glanced at the clock above the bar. Still ten minutes to go until the arranged meeting time. Brax was punctual, and if Jenna wasn't here yet, it likely meant she'd show up just in time to avoid lingering—or maybe she didn't want to risk being alone in his company for too long. Not that I blamed her.

"Chris." Smythe's voice crackled in my ear, the

faint hum of his many monitors in the background. "I've got fresh intel on Brax. You ready for it? Over."

I clicked my mic. "Go ahead, Smythe. Over."

"Turns out Brax isn't just the number two in a blood racket. He's also got his claws in something nastier—extortion using medical data from an off-the-books lab up north in Queensland. Guess who got their hands on those files? Yours truly."

"Nice work. That why Jenna's on his leash?"

"Yep. She's been feeding him patient intel in exchange for keeping her sister's existence off the radar. Brax has the kid on lockdown in some suburban shit-hole. Poor girl's only sixteen."

My grip tightened on the edge of the table. "SICB hasn't moved in yet?" The Supernatual Investigation & Crime Bureau as a whole wasn't always known for moving as quickly as they—we—could. At least in our unit, the Infiltration and Tactical Unit, we tended to be able cut through some of the red tape the government imposed on us.

"This isn't our jurisdiction, technically," Smythe admitted. "But the ITU got wind of it through a little creative digging on my part. You're welcome. Over."

I grin, "Smythe, you're the reason the SICB has increased our paycheques so damn much. Over."

"And you're the reason Michaels is rolling his eyes at me right now," Smythe quipped. "He says to tell you to quit swooning over the chef, by the way."

I froze mid-scan, my gaze flicking automatically towards the kitchen window where Waru was currently glaring at a human junior chef. Heat crept up my neck.

"I'm not swooning," I muttered into the mic. "I'm surveilling. There's a difference. Over."

"Sure there is, mate," Smythe snorted. "Michaels says he's seen less heart eyes in romcoms."

Before I could snap back, Michaels's voice cut in, dripping with faux innocence. "Don't mind me, just reminding you that Waru isn't the target here, Chris. Maybe try imagining him with spinach in his teeth? Over."

I bit back a curse, refusing to rise to the bait. Of course, that was when I felt it—a weighty gaze on me from across the room. My head angled away from Waru's hands like a magnet to find the man staring straight at me. His brow was furrowed in that perpetually pissed-off way that only added to his intensity, but his stunning amber eyes were sharp, assessing. And maybe—just maybe—a little amused.

Damn it. He'd caught me.

I offered the smallest shrug, feigning nonchalance, but he didn't look away. If anything, his lips twitched again, like he was fighting the urge to smirk outright.

Smythe's voice dragged me back to the mission. "By the way, cameras picked up your mark two streets away. Jenna's moving fast, and she's not alone. Looks like Brax sent muscle this time. Over."

"Copy that," I replied, forcing my attention back to the job. Waru's assessing gaze lingered for a second longer before he turned back to the kitchen, barking at his staff in what I was sure were clipped tones.

Still, I couldn't shake the feeling he was more than aware of the distraction he was causing. It was probably why we rarely carried out missions like this—with anyone aware of our presence. Covert ops worked best when there was no one to notice if you flinched at the wrong moment or gave away more than you intended with a stray glance. But Brax was a slippery fucker. We didn't have the luxury of waiting for the perfect setup.

Thankfully, Waru's restaurant, Kurranba, had been the ideal choice for Brax to haunt since flying in from Melbourne a week ago. Nestled on the outskirts of the city, the restaurant wasn't just close to a private airstrip—it also offered the privacy Brax preferred, thanks to Waru's refusal to open beyond his limited ten-to-four window.

He also only took reservations.

I'd done my research before approaching Waru. Kurranba, meaning *"together"* in the language of his people, the Narrunka, had been something of a revelation in Sydney's food scene. Waru had built his reputation on more than just exquisite flavours—he'd built it on connection. Every dish, from the locally sourced organic produce to the Narrunka-inspired bush tucker specials, told a story of resilience, respect, and tradition.

That's why Kurranba didn't cater to late-night crowds or all-hours socialites. Waru believed meals were meant to be shared during the day, with sunlight filtering through the tall windows and grounding you in the present. He once told a food writer that the dinner rush brought "too much noise and too little soul." That ethos, combined with his laser focus on sustainability and his razor-sharp menu, made the place wildly popular with locals and the occasional tourist who stumbled upon it.

And then there was the kitchen.

High-tech and pristine, it was Waru's domain,

but he'd grudgingly ceded the side room to me for this operation after Smythe's very convincing background pitch. The two-way mirror looking into the dining area was invaluable for surveillance—the large window in the door to my side also meant I could keep both the kitchen window and two-way mirror in my line of sight making it extra helpful since I struggle to pull my attention off Waru. I'd given Waru full assurance that my presence wouldn't disrupt his workflow.

So far, it hadn't. Unless you counted the way my gaze kept straying to him every time I caught sight of his lean figure pacing between stations, growling at his staff, or murmuring sharp commands that somehow felt like caresses. If Smythe had access to a heart monitor on me, he'd have plenty of fuel for his smug commentary.

Speaking of Smythe, his voice came back through the comms. "Chris, got another fun fact about Waru for you. Over."

I clicked the mic. "This about my distraction or his culinary brilliance? Over." Perhaps I wasn't so shy about just how much I was crushing on the man after all. *Culinary brilliance?* I should be wincing, expecting Michaels to return to comms to take the piss, but in all honesty, it had been so long since another man had captured my attention so completely, I didn't have it in me to give two shits.

"Neither. It's about why he named the place Kurranba. Apparently, it's inspired by a ceremony his community holds to honour the idea of unity—bringing people together to heal, share, and grow. Sounds like a nice concept. Over."

I could almost hear Michaels grumbling in the background about my blatant swooning. Smythe was too much of a gossip to let it slide, though. He'd seriously come into his own the last two years of working in the ITU.

"Speaking of unity, Michaels says if you and Waru keep eye flirting, we might be looking at our next SICB power couple. Over."

I groaned, my focus momentarily snapping back to Waru just as his gaze locked on mine through the door window again. His brow furrowed, lips pressing into a thin line. But was that amusement flickering there? Damn it. The man was going to kill me—one side smirk at a time.

Before I could answer Smythe, Michaels's voice broke through, dry as the Nullarbor Plain. "Chris, maybe focus on your mark. Jenna's two minutes out. Over."

I swallowed hard and tore my attention away

from the chef. Waru could wait. Right now, Brax's game was about to start, and I needed to be ready. The fact that Michaels of all people—the resident pain in the backside—had to tell me to get my head off Waru meant I really was distracted.

# 2

WARU

THE LION WAS A DISTRACTION I NEVER SAW COMING, taking my level of frustration to all new heights. My staff was feeling it, so was my oversensitive cock from me spending too many hours over the past week taking myself in hand, thinking far too explicitly about the giant, pain-in-the-arse lion who had somehow managed to needle his way under my skin.

It wasn't even like he was under my feet—staying true to his promise to keep out of my way. And since I was constantly on the move and so busy that the exhaustion seeping into my bones threatened to make me unravel, we hadn't even stood around and chitchatted.

As if I'd ever chitchat. Even if I had the time, I

had no desire to sit back and shoot the shit with anyone. Especially not an SICB agent who I'd been sharing the same space with every moment the restaurant doors were open.

Between running Kurranba and dragging my feet to let go of the reins so my new manager could step up and lighten my load—which was what I was paying them for—the only spare time I had was dedicated to my family.

Though, if you heard them tell it, they'd be more than happy for me to not spend every waking hour visiting them. Just last month, *Yayi* told me in no uncertain terms to "stop being such a miserable *gungie*" and to "go hook a man and get laid."

That was my yayi for you. She'd been like it with all her grandkids, so I had no idea why, being the youngest, I thought I would be immune to her interference. At least she wasn't trying to marry me off.

*Gungie.* I held back my snort thinking of the term. It was her go-to word for someone acting like a clueless idiot. I'd heard it muttered about some politician on the news one day and filed it away as classic Yayi. It was affectionate but sharp—a lot like her.

Still, her words echoed in my head as I slammed the oven shut and barked orders to the junior chef.

The staff were dragging today, and I couldn't blame them. My mood was fouling the air in Kurranba like a storm cloud refusing to break.

And then there was the lion, Agent Chris Flint.

Sure, he was a big guy—which was one giant tick. He also seemed competent, which may or may not have got me hard. Okay, and the not-so-subtle glances he kept casting my way were kind of a turn-on. But what really messed with my head was the Chokito bar I'd found on my desk this morning.

It wasn't there last night. No one on staff would have thought to leave me a chocolate bar—I was too much of a grumpy arsehole for that kind of thought-fulness—let alone one I'd been grumbling about not having had in ages. I didn't need to be a detective to figure out who'd left it.

Chris.

The idea that the massive lion shifter had not only overheard me but gone out of his way to track one down? It had my stomach flipping like I'd eaten raw dough. And it wasn't the *bad* kind of flip either.

Admittedly, all of those reasons told me I was lying to myself. I wasn't confused about my pull to him. He ticked a lot more than one box.

Perhaps I shouldn't think it. We were both on the job, and I could feel something dangerous brewing just below the surface in Kurranba. Brax's presence—the guy who'd somehow found his way into my restaurant and was the reason why Chris was here in the first place—had tainted the place with unease, and I hated the way my staff had picked up on it, tiptoeing around like they were waiting for something to explode.

Why the hell had I said it was okay for Chris to be here again?

My gaze flicked towards the side room where I knew he was stationed. Now wasn't the time to wonder if a man his size—all thick muscle and stunning golden eyes—would be keen to sit on my dick and let me fuck him into oblivion.

But it wasn't like I was *not* wondering either.

His muscles bunched, making me pause. Lips moving, he was clearly talking to whoever was at the other end of his earpiece. My panther hearing was phenomenal at the best of times, but the first thing the SICB had done when they took over the small room that gave almost a panoramic view of the restaurant floor was soundproof the space.

Hell, put a blind on the window in the door, and I was kinda grateful that they said I could keep the new additions. There were a lot of possibilities for what I could do with a soundproof room, especially if Chris stuck around.

I nodded at something Kira was saying, but my gaze remained firmly fixed on Chris. His head had snapped up, eyes tracking whatever was happening on the restaurant floor. Following his gaze, I peered out of the large hatch separating the kitchen from the restaurant area.

A woman entered. Human. Short and petite, she looked wary, darting furtive glances around her. At her side was a tiger shifter. My nose twitched at his scent, and unease settled in my gut. The guy was big, and while I pulled off the grump card pretty impressively, he just looked mean.

They walked towards Brax, the man Chris had told me the SICB were tracking. Brax's focus stuck to the woman, something close to distaste crossing his expression. A cruel smile appeared when he gestured to the seat before him, which she clumsily took.

Discomfort pierced my chest. This was all wrong. Everything about it.

The woman didn't want to be here. I didn't need to be a genius to figure that out. So why the hell was Chris letting this meeting take place?

"Chef."

I jerked my head towards Kira. Worry furrowed their brow. *Shit.* Just how long had they been trying to get my attention? "Yeah?" I worked hard on hiding my concern for what was happening with the meeting taking place, schooling my features in the usual "fuck off" setting.

Funnily enough, my go-to frown settled Kira immediately. Their worry disappeared.

"What's up?" I asked, crossing my arms and leaning slightly against the counter, my attention torn between the kitchen and what was bubbling in the restaurant.

"Sorry, chef," Kira said, their voice a touch hesitant. "It's just... I'm not sure the sauce for the barramundi is reducing properly. Should I add more stock, or...?"

I exhaled, dragging myself back into focus. "No stock. It's already on the thin side. Kick the heat up a touch and keep an eye on it. If it doesn't start behaving in two minutes, let me know."

Kira nodded, relief clear in their expression, and moved back to their station. I turned to the hatch and peered through again, catching a glimpse of the tiger shifter standing behind the woman, meaty hands gripping the back of her chair. His body language screamed intimidation.

Chris was still watching intently. His posture was a study in tension—bunched shoulders, clenched jaw, and hands resting too deliberately on the tabletop in the small soundproof room. When his gaze flicked towards me for half a second, I felt it like a spark down my spine.

But I didn't have time for sparks, not now. There was an hour left of service, and my team needed my focus.

"Back to it, Waru," I muttered to myself, turning my attention to the kitchen. *You can brood later.*

I walked the line, checking dishes, correcting plating, barking orders to keep everyone on track. Service was nearly over, and I could see the exhaustion setting in on my staff. They needed to push through just a little longer, and it was my job to get them there.

"Barramundi's ready, chef!" Kira called out, their voice carrying above the din.

"Run it!" I called back, giving the plate a cursory glance as it went by.

Still, my thoughts kept drifting. Something about that woman in the dining room—the way her shoulders hunched and her eyes darted like a rabbit under threat—set my instincts on edge.

Glancing back through the hatch, I saw Chris

again. He wasn't just tense anymore. His gold eyes had sharpened, his focus zeroing in on Brax and the tiger shifter. His lips moved rapidly, clearly giving orders to whoever was on the other end of his earpiece.

And then, all at once, he moved.

His chair scraped back violently, and he lunged for the door, his expression a mix of shock and barely leashed fury.

My gut twisted. Something had gone very, very wrong.

*Waru, you've got this.* I nodded to Kira as they sent out another dish, trying to stay focussed. *Service is almost done. Keep your head in the kitchen.*

But my eyes were already locked on Chris as he burst out of the soundproof room, moving with a predatory grace that sent shivers down my spine. His gaze swept the restaurant floor, and when it landed on me, I froze.

"Get everyone out of the kitchen," he said, his voice low and sharp as he crossed to the hatch covered by thick glass to ensure what happened in the kitchen stayed in the kitchen.

"What the fuck is going on?" I demanded, my own instincts flaring to life.

"Trouble," he said. "Big trouble. And it's coming this way."

# 3

CHRIS

*FUCK. FUCK. FUCCCKKKK.*

This was spiralling out of control faster than I could think. My grip tightened on the edge of the hatch lip as Smythe's voice appeared in my ear.

"Brax's boss is on her way, Flint. Prue Kole herself. She's just found out about Brax's little side hustle with that off-the-books lab in Queensland. Apparently, extorting patients and skimming from her operations was a bad call. Who knew?" Smythe's usual sardonic tone couldn't hide the tension beneath it.

I swore under my breath. Prue Kole was infamous for a reason. Ruthless didn't begin to describe her. If Brax had crossed her, there'd be hell to pay— and not just for him. The fallout could engulf Jenna,

Waru, his staff, his patrons, and anyone unlucky enough to be in Kole's crosshairs when she arrived.

"They're en route now," Smythe added, his voice grim. "You've got minutes, Chris, if we're lucky. This is a clusterfuck."

Clusterfuck didn't even cover it.

I scanned the dining room again. Jenna sat stiffly, her body language screaming discomfort. Brax leaned back in his chair, looking too smug for a man whose death warrant had likely just been signed.

And then there was Waru.

I glanced back into the kitchen to find him herding his staff towards the back exit. Relief flickered for half a second before my gut clenched. Waru's sharp gaze locked on me, and I knew with a sinking certainty he wasn't planning to make a clean getaway.

He had people on the floor, both staff and patrons. I'd seen his type before—stubborn, protective, and unwilling to abandon anyone under his care. I didn't know whether to admire him or throttle him for it.

"Smythe," I said through gritted teeth, keeping my voice low as I moved towards the side door, "I need orders. Now."

"Lucas is coming on," Smythe replied. A moment later, my boss's calm, authoritative voice filled my ear.

"Chris, listen up. Shaw, Michaels, and Smythe are already staged a block away. Eclipse Security is inbound with three vehicles. They'll be there in under five."

Five minutes. We didn't have five minutes.

"I'm pulling Brax and Jenna out," I said quickly, my gaze flicking back to the dining room. "Brax might take the deal. He's got enough brains to know it's his only shot at survival. But if Kole gets here before I move them—"

"She won't," Lucas cut in firmly. "Your priority is keeping civilians safe. Get Brax and Jenna out if you can, but don't risk the restaurant."

Easy for him to say. He wasn't here, staring at a dining room full of unsuspecting people about to be caught in the crossfire.

"Understood," I said tightly, though the words tasted like ash.

And then I caught Waru's movement again. He was back on the floor, weaving through the tables and speaking in low tones to his staff. Quietly, efficiently, he was clearing out as many people as he could without raising alarm.

My fear spiked as I realized what that meant. Waru wasn't running. He was staying, likely to deal with whatever fallout hit his restaurant.

"Damn it," I muttered, reaching for the hatch door.

"Chris?" Lucas asked sharply.

"Waru's not leaving," I said.

There was a beat of silence.

"Keep him alive," Lucas ordered finally. "Team's almost there. Don't engage unless you have no choice."

A burst of static followed as Michaels's voice chimed in. "For the record, Waru staying behind doesn't surprise me. Stubborn chef. Hot chef. Kind of fits his whole vibe, doesn't it?"

"Not the time, Michaels," I snapped.

"Oh, but it is. You're making *that* face again, Chris."

I ignored him and the fact he must be staring at me through the camera feed and pushed through the hatch, my focus narrowing on Waru. He turned as I approached, his jaw set and his eyes blazing with that fierce determination that looked far too hot on him.

"We're clearing out the staff," he said before I could open my mouth. "But I've got patrons still on the floor. I'm not leaving until everyone's safe."

I stepped closer, lowering my voice. "Waru, this isn't your fight. Kole's not someone you want to cross. If she gets here—"

"If she gets here, I'll deal with it," he interrupted, his tone clipped.

"No, you won't," I said sharply. "You don't know what you're dealing with. Kole's not just dangerous—she's lethal. If you stay, you're putting everyone here in even more danger."

His gaze hardened, but I didn't miss the flicker of fear beneath the defiance.

"I'm not leaving them," he said firmly.

And damn it, I knew he meant it.

*Fuck.* I had to move. I leaned in close to Waru, close enough that I could feel his warmth, smell the faint, clean scent of him that made my chest tighten. Steel hardened my voice. "You stay safe. You stay away from the front windows. And so fucking help me, if you die before I get the chance to finally kiss you, I'm going to kick your arse."

His breath hitched, red touching his cheeks, but I spun around quickly, unable to make good on the desire pulsing through me to capture his lips with mine.

The tiger was my target. Incapacitate but not maim, plus I needed him to walk out of here. Me carrying the man out wasn't on my bingo card tonight.

I moved fast, crossing the space between the kitchen and the restaurant floor in measured, deliberate strides. My focus zeroed in on the tiger shifter now standing at Brax's side. He was tall, broad, and looked like he bench-pressed small cars for fun—but big didn't mean fast. I'd dealt with his type before.

"Agent Flint," Waru hissed behind me, but I didn't slow. "Chris" followed, but there was no turning back.

The tiger shifter didn't catch my movement until I was already on him. My elbow slammed into his solar plexus, driving the air from his lungs with a wheezing grunt. Before he could recover, I pivoted behind him, locking his arms in a vice grip and sweeping his legs out from under him. He went down hard, the crack of the floorboards echoing as his head smacked against them.

Jenna screamed, the sharp sound cutting through the restaurant like a blade. Brax flinched, paling so rapidly, I thought he might pass out on the spot.

The tiger writhed beneath me, his growls of anger quickly turning to pained snarls as I pressed a knee into his spine, keeping him pinned. "Don't move," I ordered, voice flat and uncompromising.

The tiger froze. Smart move.

I glanced up, locking eyes with Brax. The man was trembling so badly, I could see his hands shaking where they gripped the edge of the table.

"Here's how this works, Brax," I said coldly. "You're coming with me. You're going to spill every goddamn piece of intel you have on Prue Kole and her network. Every name, every location, every transaction. You give us what we need, and you might just walk out of this alive."

"Might?" His voice cracked.

I bared my teeth in a humourless grin. "Might. If you don't take the deal, here's what happens: I arrest you, drag your sorry ass in, and you get to watch Kole's people take you apart piece by piece once you're sent down. Or option three—you end up dead right here. Your call."

Brax swallowed hard, sweat gleaming on his forehead. "I... I—"

"Make up your mind," I snapped. "You're out of time, Brax. Kole's on her way right now. Looks like she's heard about your side hustle." He paled further at my words.

I was aware of every detail around me: the tiger shifter's shallow breaths, Jenna's trembling hands as she edged away from the table, and Waru.

God, Waru.

Even now, as chaos brewed around him, he was a rock. His voice carried low and soothing as he guided patrons out of the restaurant through the kitchen, ushering them towards safety with calm authority. He didn't bark orders or panic; he exuded a quiet command that made people trust him, follow him without question.

I shouldn't have been watching him. My attention should've been fully on Brax and the tiger. But I couldn't help it. The way he moved, the way he handled the situation with unshakable poise—it was magnetic.

I scented Michaels and Shaw before I spotted them. I didn't glance over, knowing they were in the kitchen, ushering out the last of the civilians.

"Fine!" Brax's voice cracked, pulling me back to the moment. "I'll take the deal! Just get me out of here!"

I gave him a sharp nod. "Good choice."

Behind me, I heard the click of the rear door as

the last patron exited. Waru was back, moving closer.

I stood, dragging the tiger up with me. He groaned but didn't resist as I twisted his arm behind his back and pushed him towards the kitchen just as Michaels entered, Shaw on his six.

Shaw immediately put the tiger in cuffs, giving me the chance to reach out for Brax while Michaels focussed on Jenna and Waru. The man in my grip continued to tremble, his gaze darting this way and that.

Time was running—

"Incoming." Smythe's voice filtered through comms, causing all agents' muscles to pull taut.

"Fuck," Michaels groaned. "Smythe, is the rear exit still clear? Copy."

If it wasn't, we'd be royally screwed. My gaze darted to Waru, the only civilian not in custody. He'd paused at Michaels's outburst, a mask of worry forming on his expression. When he flicked his attention to me, an unspoken question filled his gaze.

*Just how screwed are we?*

Pretty sure the panther was having a whole lot of regrets at the moment, with him welcoming us into his restaurant no doubt being at the top of the list.

"That's an affirmative. Kitchen exit is clear. Eclipse is thirty seconds out. Copy."

"Let's move," I instructed as soon as Smythe gave us the all clear. We raced for the exit, Shaw in front with the tiger, Michaels with Brax ahead of me, while I took up the rear, hot on the heels of Jenna and Waru.

He didn't say a word, even as we made it through the exit. I didn't think I'd seen stoic look so hot. But again, so not the time.

As we emptied the kitchen, the cooling spring afternoon air greeted us. Movement to my right caught my attention. I reached for my gun, tugging it out of my holster with speed.

"Eclipse vehicles are approaching round back," Smythe said, just as the screech of tyres and brakes reached us from the front of the building. "SUV has split from Kole's formation. They'll be on you in ten seconds."

Shaw was already tugging his SUV door open and shoving Brax's bodyguard inside before there was fully room. The tiger cursed as his head smacked against the frame, but that didn't stop Shaw from manhandling him inside. What was it about panthers that made them such feisty fuckers? I'd have to ask Michaels another time—ideally when we weren't about to be shot at—what it was like dating Shaw, a panther shifter.

Michaels reached the open door, forcing Brax inside while Shaw got behind the wheel and started the engine.

"You take Jenna and Waru. Go with Eclipse." Michaels jumped into the SUV beside Shaw. "Meet you at Stilton," he shouted before slamming the door shut. Not even a split second later, Shaw gunned it, leaving me to reach for Jenna and all but drag her towards Jimmy, who'd stepped out of the lead Eclipse vehicle armed and waiting for us.

Jimmy met us with a cocky grin that didn't quite mask the sharp readiness in his eyes. His rifle—yes, rifle... like who the fuck used a rifle these days unless they were on a range?—was slung casually over his shoulder, but his stance screamed alertness. He gave me a once-over as I pushed Jenna towards him.

"Nice of you to join us, Chris. Thought you might've been too busy playing house in there," he quipped.

"Can it, Jimmy," I shot back, my voice clipped, not even surprised he'd been pulled into gossip.

"You've got orders to get them to Stilton. You clear on that?"

"Crystal." He nodded, his grin widening. "Hop in, princess. Let the professionals handle this."

I had to bite back a retort as he opened the door for Jenna, helping her inside with a flourish that bordered on theatrical. She flinched at the sound of a distant gunshot, but he was quick to calm her.

"Don't worry, love," he said, his tone surprisingly gentle. "You're safer with me than a nun in a church."

Behind us, the screech of tyres pulled my attention. An SUV swerved around the corner, and my stomach tightened when I saw the muzzle flash.

Gunfire cracked through the air.

"Move!" I barked, reaching for my weapon.

Jimmy was already shoving Jenna fully into the vehicle, snapping the door shut before diving behind the engine block for cover. The next bullet slammed into the side of the SUV, inches from where he'd been standing.

"We've gotta go!" Jimmy shouted, his voice tinged with urgency.

I turned, grabbing Waru by the wrist, intent on dragging him to safety. But he didn't budge. Instead, he pulled me, nodding towards a side lot.

"My car's closer!" he shouted over the chaos.

I hesitated. Leaving the convoy went against every instinct, but the logic was sound. Waru's vehicle was parked out of sight, and I trusted him to know the layout better than anyone.

"Fine," I snapped, already moving with him.

The lot was tucked away under cover, the dim light casting deep shadows that only made my nerves prickle further. Waru's grip was firm, and he moved with a purpose that belied the danger we were in.

"There." He pointed to a sleek black sedan tucked into the corner.

As soon as we reached the car, he released my hand and unlocked it with a press of his fob. The doors clicked open, and I didn't waste time jumping in.

"You drive," I ordered Waru, my voice leaving no room for argument.

He raised a brow, looking like he wanted to argue anyway, but slid into the driver's seat.

Jimmy's voice crackled over the comms in my ear. "Second SUV just pulled up. Eclipse has them pinned, but Kole's got more coming your way."

"Copy," I replied, climbing into the passenger

seat and slamming the door shut. "Jimmy, get moving. We'll meet you at Stilton."

"Don't have to tell me twice," he shot back through comms.

Waru's hands gripped the wheel tightly as he pulled out of the lot, his movements smooth and practiced.

"You good to drive under fire?" I asked, watching his profile as we sped away.

He gave me a side-eye glance, equal parts exasperation and pride. "I didn't grow up with eighteen cousins, all older and twice as feral, without learning to handle myself. Running for cover? That's child's play compared to family reunions."

A grin tugged at my lips despite the tension. Damn, this man was something else.

Behind us, the sound of gunfire faded as we turned onto the main road. But I wasn't naïve enough to think we were in the clear.

"Keep your foot down," I said, my gaze scanning the rearview mirror.

"Already on it," Waru replied, his focus razor-sharp as he navigated the streets.

As we sped further from the restaurant, my mind raced. Lucas was going to go apeshit that it had all got so out of control. Thank fuck for Eclipse stepping in. It would likely mean reaching out to Callen, too, the division head. And that was all that we needed: another joker in the mix who would probably say that this was my plan all along—to steal Waru away and get him alone.

I wasn't even exaggerating.

Waru might have eighteen cousins he had to wrangle. Me? I had a unit, a security team, and a division head who were absolutely my family. And as one of the few single guys left, I regularly had their full attention as they took every opportunity they could to interfere and meddle with my life.

I'd hate the fuckers if I didn't love them so damn much.

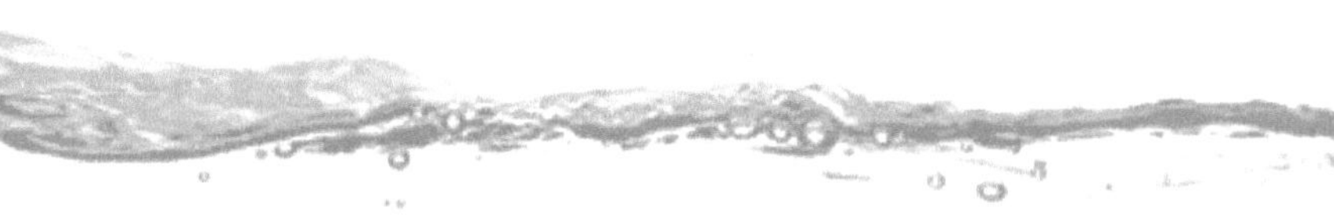

# 4

WARU

The frantic beating of my heart should have been enough for me to hyperventilate. If I wasn't so good in a crisis, that would be exactly what I was doing.

"Waru, you're good to ease off the accelerator."

I got the impression that wasn't the first time Chris had said those words to me, making me rethink just how "good in a crisis" I really was. Heaving out a breath before inhaling slowly, I inch my foot back, my car slowing down. For about ten minutes I'd been driving directionless, just wanting to get out of there, away from flying bullets. A glance around had me frowning.

"You doing okay?" Chris's voice was a deep caress and surprisingly grounding. All this time I kept my shit together, not freaking out or letting my panic spiral, but from the trembling in my hands, any semblance of calm was going to go flying out of the window. "Waru, pull over here." He reached over, flicking my indicator to pull into the quiet pub car park. Another hour or so and the tradies would no doubt fill the space for their final beer of the day after work before heading home.

Pulling into a space, I sighed on another exhale before putting my car into Park. My belt was unclipped for me, but it was the warm hand that had me unclenching my grip on the wheel.

"You did great. You got us out of there safely."

I nodded at his words, trying to silence the what-ifs as I did so.

"We'll just take a breather, and then we'll get moving, yeah?" His strong palm squeezed my forearm, dragging my attention to his sun-kissed skin covered by a smattering of blond hairs. They were almost the shade of his short locks, but the hints of red cut through the sunshine yellow.

"Yeah. Okay?" I made to switch off the engine, but Chris stopped me.

"Let's leave it on."

*Fuck.* The "just in case" went unsaid.

The quiet in the car stretched taut, tension clinging to the air like the remnants of gunpowder.

My hands rested on my thighs, finally still, though my chest still rose and fell in an unsteady rhythm.

"Waru," Chris said again, softer this time. My name on his lips was almost a plea.

I turned my head towards him, intending to reassure him that I was fine. Really. But whatever words I was about to say evaporated. His gaze locked on mine, and the unspoken intensity in his golden eyes was a tether I couldn't break.

Before I could second-guess myself—or before Chris could—I leaned forwards, closing the space between us.

The moment our lips met, it was like a fuse had been lit. A heady mix of relief, adrenaline, and raw chemistry exploded between us. His hand cradled my jaw, thumb brushing the curve of my cheek, while I angled towards him, swallowing the quiet groan he let slip.

God, he tasted good—like coffee, like danger, like the spark of something I hadn't let myself hope for.

It wasn't soft or sweet. It was frantic, consuming, a desperate clash of mouths and teeth that made me forget the bullets, the fear, and everything else except him.

When we finally pulled apart, our breaths

mingling in the confined space, I felt more grounded than I had in hours. My lips tingled, and the sharp edges of the world seemed a little softer.

Chris didn't apologise, and neither did I. His gaze lingered on my mouth for a beat longer before he cleared his throat.

"We need to go," he said, though his voice was rougher than I'd started getting used to.

I nodded, still reeling but pulling it together. "Where?"

"To Stilton," he said, easing back into his professional veneer, though the flush on his neck betrayed him. "It's a safe house, about an hour south of Sydney. It's where we'll be holding the people we've arrested."

I frowned. "Why do I need to go? Why can't I just head home?"

His lips pressed into a thin line, and he hesitated for a moment before answering, "Because you're a witness now. And because I don't trust Kole's people not to retaliate."

The mention of Kole sent a chill through me, but I worked to push it down. I should be worried about my staff, about the restaurant, about the damage and what condition it was in. But as my yayi always told me, "You've got to listen to the land, to what your gut tells you."

And right now? My gut was screaming not to let Chris out of my sight.

"You're driving," he said suddenly, pulling me out of my thoughts.

I blinked. "What?"

He gestured to the car. "Your car's less conspicuous than anything Eclipse has got. And honestly, I'm not sure I trust anyone else to keep us in one piece right now."

My throat tightened at the compliment, but I rolled my eyes for show. "Fine. But if we get pulled over for speeding, you're the one explaining it to the cop."

Chris chuckled, low and deep, as his hand settled on my thigh. It was a possessive touch, reassuring and grounding all at once.

I didn't question it.

Didn't move it.

Hell, I didn't even think I *could*.

But focusing on the road while his fingers rested there? That was a challenge I wasn't prepared for, but I'd give it a good go.

We drove with Chris spending most of the time talking through his comms. Picking up half a conversation was all levels of frustrating, but likewise, the less information I had, the sooner I could return to normality when all this was over.

"Is this the norm for you? Your life? Dodging bullets?" I asked when he'd signed off with "Over and out" a few minutes ago. We were almost forty minutes out of the city, traffic not too bad considering it was a Sunday.

I shot a look his way when I felt him do the same. A gentle squeeze of my leg preceded his "It's not an everyday occurrence." There was a brief hesitation before he said, "Sometimes there's a case that makes things... tricky."

I somehow held back my snort at his word choice. Tricky? Tricky was timing the rising of a soufflé to perfection, not going through your day wondering if you were going to get shot. At least that was the case in my world.

"And while there's always a case that needs working on and there's often an arrest on the horizon, I can hand on heart say that last time I was shot at was seven months ago."

My brows jumped high, and I whipped my head in his direction. His "you see how awesome I am because it's been a whole seven months" smile dropped, no doubt at seeing my expression. I bounced between incredulous that he thought that was an impressive length of time and horror that he was basically saying at least, what… twice a year someone tried to kill him?

"Uhm…." He trailed off, no longer looking so certain.

"*That* is absolutely not normal." I shook my head, an uncomfortable churning in my gut starting at him being at risk. "You know that, right?"

After a beat, he squeezed my thigh once more, but this time I lost his touch as he slowly removed his hand. My gut bottomed out, already feeling the drift before we'd had a chance to get started.

His expression shifted, not quite softening, but transforming into almost a careful understanding. "I get why you'd think that, and you're right, it shouldn't be normal for anyone. In an ideal world, we'd all be going about our daily lives smelling the roses, chasing rainbows, and fucking under the stars."

My heart flipped at his words. All of that sounded like heaven. Where could I sign up for that with him?

But he wasn't finished. He continued calmly, the only inflection evident one of quiet understanding, "But that's not the world we live in. We're imperfect.

Humans, supes, people in power, folks who should know better—every single one of us is flawed." He searched my gaze, staring at me with his golden eyes that looked so much darker in the dimming light. "It's my job to do what I can to make things better. To hold people accountable when they step out of line. To stop the bad guys from ruining the good parts of life for the rest of us."

His words carried weight, but his voice remained steady, almost serene. He wasn't just explaining himself—he was grounding me, calming the churning storm of worry inside me.

"That's... noble," I said, trying to sound less rattled than I felt.

Chris gave me a wry smile. "Noble's one way to put it. Frustrating, exhausting, and sometimes downright maddening are others."

I huffed out a laugh despite myself, the corners of my mouth twitching upwards.

"Still," he added, his tone softening as his gaze zeroed in on my lips before he made eye contact, "I wouldn't trade it for anything. It's who I am. But I get that it's not easy to hear."

His words left me warm, conflicted. Was he trying to warn me? Or prepare me?

"And what about relationships?" The question

slipped out before I could stop it, my voice quieter than I'd intended.

The corner of his mouth quirked up. "That's a big question."

"Yeah, well, I'm a curious kind of guy."

That earned me a chuckle, but the smile faded into something more thoughtful. "It's complicated," he admitted, his focus shifting back to the road. "Most of my friends in the bureau—and even in Eclipse—they tend to date other agents or people in similar lines of work. It makes sense when you think about it."

"Because no one else would want to put up with the danger?" I asked, only half-joking.

"Partly," he said, his smile returning faintly. "But mostly because they understand. They know what it's like to drop everything for a call. To live with uncertainty. To carry the weight of a world that never really stops spinning."

His explanation made sense, but it didn't make me feel any better. My gut twisted, and I stared out the window, watching the blur of cars as they drove past us.

Was he telling me we couldn't explore this thing between us? That I wasn't cut out for his life?

"Waru," he said gently, pulling my gaze back to

him. "That's not me saying this can't happen. I just wanted to be upfront with you about why people like me end up where we do."

I blinked at him, my pulse quickening. "Then what are you saying?"

He held my gaze a beat longer before answering, "I'm saying that while my job can be consuming, I don't want it to be my whole life. When I clock off, I want to spend time with someone who reminds me there's a world outside all of this. Someone who makes me laugh. Who doesn't care about badges or agencies. Someone who's got a life of their own and is okay letting me be part of it."

The weight in my chest eased, but my heart was still racing, the touch of our kiss replaying in my mind. Was he saying...?

Something in his words chipped away at the barriers I'd spent years building. I'd learned to wear my edges sharp, my front unyielding, like stone worn smooth by storms. But Chris didn't look at me like I was all hardness. He saw the part of me I tried to forget—the softer core I couldn't quite carve out, no matter how many layers I wrapped it in.

"Chris," I said quietly, my voice almost unrecognisable to my own ears. "Are you sure you're ready to deal with someone like me? I'm not exactly known for making life easy." Jesus, just ask any of my staff or my family. The latter loved me unconditionally, but I knew it wasn't always easy for them.

"I—" His hand went to his ear, signalling someone was speaking. "Copy that," he said into the receiver. "ETA twenty minutes."

The moment was gone, replaced by the distant hum of urgency that seemed to linger around him.

Chris turned back to me, his expression calm but determined. "We should get a move on."

I nodded and focussed fully on the road ahead, accelerating a little, driving towards a destination that was still unclear in more ways than one.

As the road stretched on, I couldn't stop thinking about what he'd said. About what he hadn't said.

Was I being reckless even thinking about pursuing something with a man like Chris?

Maybe.

But damn, I wanted to.

# 5

## CHRIS

Perhaps kissing a civilian while running for our lives wasn't the best-thought-out decision I'd ever made, but it was so worth it. I'd managed to pull a full smile from him. That was leagues above a barely there twitch of the lips.

What I needed to do was focus, especially as we pulled up at the safe house. Callen would be pissed I'd let Waru drive rather than hooding him. It would mean shutting the place down after this. Apparently, I was full of questionable decisions today.

We parked around the back after another loop, my focus not straying from the wing mirror—not that I technically needed to, as Smythe had already given me the all clear.

Waru turned off the engine and peered at me. Nerves danced in his gaze, and he swallowed hard, the audible click sounding loud in the cab of the car.

I shouldn't... I really, really shouldn't have, but I reached out and took his hand in mine. The first time we'd been dodging bullets, so I hadn't had time to commit to memory his elegant fingers or how much I liked the fit of his palm in mine.

"When we head in," I started quietly, "the first thing that'll happen is you'll be checked out. Make sure you didn't pick up any scrapes."

His brow jumped high. "Any scrapes I might have got would be healed by now."

"True." Our shifter healing meant fast healing. "But humour me, yeah? It's just protocol." What I didn't explain was that there were several advanced weapons out there that could cause some serious damage to shifters and vampires. A simple nick from a treated flying bullet had the potential to cause serious infection. That wasn't information the SICB or the government wanted to be common knowledge.

"Okay. And then what?"

I kept my tone light, concern growing in my gut as he started to flag before me. "We'll get you set up with something to eat and drink before the adrenaline crash really kicks in. Then you'll be asked a few questions. After that, you'll be all done."

"I'll be fine. I don't need to—"

I cut him off, not wanting to call bullshit, but I figured he hadn't noticed the trembling in his hands. "I know you'll be fine." He pursed his lips. "We'll just follow the process, okay?"

A sigh escaped his parted lips, followed by a nod.

"Let's get this done." Reluctantly, I released his hand before getting out of his car. I'd already clocked Michaels's SUV and the van we used for tech support that Smythe must have driven back. There was only one Eclipse vehicle in sight.

I led the way and typed in the code when I reached the door, then placed my thumb against the reader. The door unlocked, and we stepped into a small holding area. Once I closed the door behind us, I reached the retina scanner, passed, then typed in a secondary code via the security app Lucas had designed.

The final door opened, the quiet grinding highlighting just how thick the steel door was. Yeah, Callen was not going to be a happy bunny about giving up this safe house.

Once inside, I took a moment to gauge Waru's reaction to the space.

The main room stretched before us, open and inviting despite its purpose. Warm wood tones and soft lighting made the sitting area feel almost cosy, with a pair of plush couches positioned around a low coffee table. The dining area flowed seamlessly into a sleek, modern kitchen. The counter was quartz, polished to a high sheen, and every appliance looked like it belonged in a high-end showroom.

"Wow," Waru muttered, his eyes darting around the space. "This is not what I expected."

"Yeah?" I asked, amused.

He nodded, gesturing vaguely at the room. "It's... homey. Not what I'd picture for a safe house."

I chuckled. "Lucas likes his comforts, and Callen believes in good morale. Happy team, effective team, or something like that." Which was all bullshit. The truth was that after a major criminal takedown we were involved in a couple of years back, a whole lot of shit happened, and damage had been done. Our budget since then had been super healthy.

Waru's lips twitched, a spark of levity in his expression. "Still feels weird."

Before I could answer, the sound of the entryway

door cycling through the locks preceded Michaels's arrival. He strode in with his usual casual confidence, a grin plastered on his face as he caught sight of us.

"Chris," Michaels greeted, giving me a firm handshake before pulling me into a brief hug. His tone was all professional, but his smile turned downright mischievous as he turned to Waru.

"And you must be Waru." Michaels extended his hand. "Michaels. It's nice to meet you properly. We didn't really have time for introductions earlier."

Waru hesitated for a fraction of a second before taking Michaels's hand.

"Likewise," Waru said, though his eyes darted nervously towards me.

Michaels's grin widened. "Don't worry. We're just going to get you checked out real quick. Standard protocol." He gestured towards the room off to the side of the pantry.

Waru glanced at me again, clearly searching for reassurance. "I'll be right here," I said, giving him a slight nod. "You're in good hands."

Michaels clapped him on the shoulder lightly, guiding him towards the medical room.

Once they disappeared through the door, I exhaled and headed towards the back. The hallway led to the more secure parts of the safe house. Three bedrooms, each behind reinforced doors with their own keypads, lined one side. On the other were doors leading to the holding cells and the interview room.

Lucas was waiting for me near the farthest door.

The vampire looked as unflappable as ever, his sharp features softened slightly by the calm confidence he radiated. A faint smirk curved his lips as he spotted me.

"Chris," he greeted, his voice smooth.

"Boss man." I returned the nod before stepping closer, sure in his head he was rolling his eyes at me. He wasn't a fan of being called boss man.

"How's our guest?"

"Shaken but holding up," I said. "Michaels is with him now, running through the protocol."

Lucas nodded, then gestured for me to follow him into the back office. Once the door clicked shut behind us, he leaned against the desk.

"Updates?" I asked.

"Jenna will be transferred after her interview," Lucas said. "Another unit is handling her and her sister. Brax is... predictably pathetic. He's giving us enough, but it's clear he was a puppet, not a player.

And as for the tiger...." He grimaced. "Annoying as hell, but reluctantly cooperative."

I snorted. "No surprise there."

Lucas tilted his head, studying me. "This case isn't going to be ours for much longer. Callen's on his way, and he's made it clear this is being shifted to another team."

Frustration curled in my gut, but I kept my face neutral. "Figures. We were dragged into this mess, and now they're pulling us out."

Lucas's smirk returned. "Bright side? A few days off."

I grunted in response, though the thought of some downtime wasn't unappealing.

"Anything else I need to know?" I asked.

"Not for now." Lucas straightened. "Focus on getting Waru through this."

I nodded, the weight of the case fading slightly as I left the office.

Waru's well-being was my priority now.

It took four hours before I could get Waru out of there and home safely. Since eating and his interview, he was at the point of crashing. His eyes were heavy, almost glazed and unfocussed. While the calories had picked him up a little, what energy he'd stored was almost gone.

He didn't even put up a fight about me driving him home in his car.

I stared at him for a moment, taking in the wide set of his nose, the gentle slope of his cheekbones, and the way his dark lashes fanned against his skin. His lips were slightly parted, and the soft rise and fall of his chest was a soothing rhythm. Even with the tension of the day weighing him down, there was an innocence in his expression, as though sleep had granted him a brief escape from reality.

The urge to let him rest battled with the knowledge that he'd be more comfortable inside.

"Waru," I said softly, reaching out to gently touch his shoulder.

He stirred, scrunching his nose before his eyes fluttered open. For a moment, he blinked at me in confusion, his gaze struggling to focus.

"You're home," I murmured, smiling despite myself.

"Oh." His voice was groggy, and he rubbed at his face before yawning. "Right. Home."

I opened the car door and walked around to his side, pulling his door open. Waru fumbled with the seatbelt for a second before I reached in to help him. He blinked up at me, still a little dazed, and let out a quiet laugh. "Guess I'm out of it, huh?"

"Come on, sleepyhead," I teased, offering my hand to help him out.

Waru's house was small and modest, but there was a warmth to it that suited him. I led him to the door, and when we stepped inside, I hesitated. His nerves were palpable, his steps slowing as the reality of the day seemed to catch up with him.

"You okay?" I asked softly.

He looked at me, his eyes shadowed with worry. "I... I don't know. It's just... a lot."

"I can arrange security," I offered. "They can sit outside, keep an eye on the place."

Waru hesitated, his brow furrowing. "It all happened at the restaurant, though," he said, his voice cracking slightly. "What about my staff? My restaurant?"

"They're fine," I assured him. "The SICB secured the place and checked on everyone. Your staff is safe, and the restaurant is locked up tight."

The tension visibly drained from his shoulders, and he sagged against me, his forehead pressing into my chest. Instinctively, I wrapped my arms around him, holding him close. His warmth seeped into me, and I felt his breath hitch against my shirt.

"You need to sleep," I murmured.

He nodded against me, his voice muffled. "Yeah. I do." He pulled back just enough to look up at me, his eyes vulnerable but steady. "Stay?"

I hesitated. "Waru...."

"Not like that," he added quickly, a faint flush creeping into his cheeks. "I just... I don't want to be alone."

After a beat, I nodded. "Okay. But I'll take the couch."

His frown deepened, and he shook his head. "No. You'll take the bed."

"Waru—"

He grabbed my hand and tugged me towards what I assumed was his room with surprising determination. "The bed," he repeated firmly, leaving no chance for argument. Not that I wanted to.

In his bedroom, he didn't waste time, stripping down to his boxers before turning to me with expectant eyes. "You too."

I couldn't help but laugh softly. "You're bossy when you're tired."

He raised an eyebrow, and I relented, tugging off my shirt and jeans before climbing into the bed.

Waru didn't hesitate, curling up against me like a koala. He was all warmth, his head resting on my chest and one arm slung across my torso.

"Goodnight, Chris," he mumbled, his voice heavy with exhaustion.

"Goodnight, Waru," I whispered.

In less than ten seconds, he was asleep, his soft breathing a balm to the chaos of the day.

# 6

WARU

Hair tickled my nose. I moved my face left to right, trying to scratch and stop the tickle. Warm skin, sweet-smelling sweat… lion. Chris.

Stilling, I tuned into his heartbeat, right next to where my face was pressed against his barrel chest. A steady thump didn't clue me into whether he was awake or not, so I focussed on his breathing.

One exhale. Two.

"I can hear you thinking." The deep rumble of his voice wrapped around me. Goose bumps sprang to life, covering my arms quicker than I could fully appreciate his scent or the position I'd woken in.

As I debated whether to move or not, Chris's strong, bare arms enveloped me. My breath caught before I melted against him, happy for him to make the decision for the two of us.

"Have you been awake long?" I asked, my voice gravelly and rough with sleep. From the faint light spilling into my bedroom, dawn had not long broken, maybe for an hour or so from the brightness of the room.

"Not really. Maybe fifteen minutes or so."

I nodded against his chest, enjoying how his hair rubbed my cheek. It had been a long time since I'd shared a bed with anyone. Since opening Kurranba seven years ago, life had been all work and fairly limited play. Sure, in the last couple of years I'd made a greater effort to find balance by staying closed on Mondays and hiring a manager who I still hadn't allowed to take the reins, but balance still felt out of reach.

Maybe if I had someone who encouraged me to take time out and reminded me the world existed away from the restaurant, that would be all the push I'd need. Maybe.

"You're not at work today, right?"

"No," I answered, finally building the courage to angle my head a little to peer up at him, albeit awkwardly. "Do you need to get going?" In my exhausted state yesterday, I thought he mentioned having a couple days off, but I couldn't be certain. The past week had been stressful. The past twelve hours had been... hell, they'd been tense as fuck and dove right into being traumatic.

He shook his head, his lips pressing against my forehead before I could process. My brows shot high, but if Chris thought his kissing me was odd, then he didn't show it. Instead, a slow smile formed as he angled to see me better. "I'm all yours for the day if you don't have plans and want me to stay."

I blinked up at him, caught between my usual composure and the way my body buzzed with awareness. Chris's smile was lazy, content, and devastatingly sexy. I was pretty sure I looked like I'd just fallen out of a gum tree.

"I, uh...," I stammered, heat creeping into my cheeks. "Yeah. That'd be nice."

His arms tightened around me slightly, and the motion pressed me closer to the hard planes of his chest. I became acutely aware of his warmth, the solidness of his body, and the way his scent—earthy, with a faint hint of spice—wrapped around me like a blanket.

Then I realised exactly how draped over him I

was. My legs tangled with his, my torso flush against his, and, fuck, my morning wood pressed uncomfortably close to his thigh.

Awareness shot through me, and before I could control it, my cock swelled further, throbbing against the hard muscle of his leg. My breath caught. I tried to shift away subtly, but the motion only made things worse.

Chris's eyes dropped, his gaze drifting down my body. Heat flared in his golden eyes, slow and intense. He didn't say a word for a long moment, just looked, and my heart threatened to burst out of my chest.

"Chris, I—" I started, scrambling for an apology.

"Give me your hand," he said, his voice quiet but filled with a rough command that sent a shiver down my spine.

I froze, staring at him. The air between us was thick, tension bubbling just under the surface, ready to snap. Slowly, I lifted my hand and placed it in his.

His fingers curled around mine, warm and sure, and he guided me downwards, under the sheet. He moved slowly, giving me plenty of time to pull back if I wanted to. I didn't.

When my palm brushed against his cock, thick

and hot, I swallowed hard. My brain short-circuited, and all I could do was hold him, feel the solid weight of him against my hand.

"Chris," I whispered, his name a mix of reverence and desperation.

He didn't reply. He didn't have to. The way he looked at me, like I was the only thing that mattered, stole my breath.

I yanked the sheet back, exposing him fully, and tugged his boxers down. His cock sprang free, impressive and perfect. I wasn't one to focus on size, but Chris was all thick length and weight, and my mouth watered at the sight.

"Off," he said, his voice rough with desire, and his gaze flicked to my boxers.

I didn't hesitate, pushing them down and kicking them off. The way he groaned, low and appreciative, sent a thrill through me.

Before I could act on the desperate urge to take him in my mouth, he grabbed me, his hand firm on the back of my neck, and pulled me into a kiss. His lips were soft but demanding, and his tongue teased mine until I was dizzy.

When he broke the kiss, I barely had time to catch my breath before he shifted me effortlessly, his strength undeniable. He spun me around, pulling me into a 69 position.

I didn't have time to be self-conscious before his mouth was on me, hot and wet and sending jolts of pleasure through my body.

"Oh, fuck," I gasped, my hands gripping his hips for balance.

I returned the favour, taking him into my mouth as best as I could. He groaned around me, the vibrations pushing me closer to the edge.

Tentatively, I let one hand drift lower, brushing against the tight ring of muscle at his entrance. I hesitated, unsure, but when he shifted his hips, opening for me, I pressed a spit-slick finger inside.

He moaned, the sound wrecked and beautiful, and I couldn't get enough... of him, his arse, this moment. I sucked hard as I drove one, then two fingers inside his channel. He gripped my fingers. Fuck, with Chris around my cock, I'd be in heaven given half the chance.

He gripped my hips, yanking me deeper and so far into his throat, I saw stars. I shuddered, my body trembling while I tried to focus enough to make him come undone. Sucking my cheeks in, I went for the kill shot. I pulled him into my mouth, held my breath, and swallowed around his length.

Chris tensed, gripping me so hard and perfectly, I'd wear his bruises.

When he came, spilling hot and thick into my mouth, his body went pliant against mine. Still sucking me down, his movements slow but thorough, he tugged my balls, sending bright relief into my vision as I came long and hard, shooting ribbons of cum down his convulsing throat.

We collapsed side by side, breathing heavily, our limbs tangled.

I stared at him, dazed and completely wrecked. "Chris," I said softly, "I think I need to call my manager."

His brow quirked. "Oh?"

I grinned, brushing a hand over his chest as I turned myself around to be closer to his face. "I was supposed to do a stock take today, but spending the day in bed with you sounds a hell of a lot better."

His laugh rumbled through me, low and warm, and I knew I'd made the right choice.

---

"So," Chris began, leaning back in his chair and wiping the corner of his mouth with a napkin, "who taught you to cook? What made you fall in love with it?"

I didn't answer right away, too caught up in watching him. His plate was nearly clean—a testament to the barramundi I'd pan seared with lemon myrtle butter, served alongside a roasted beet and macadamia salad and a pepperberry-infused damper roll.

He ate like it was the first time he'd tasted food, his every movement deliberate. The way his fork lifted the last flake of fish to his mouth, or how his tongue darted out to catch a stray drop of butter clinging to his bottom lip—it was foreplay on a level I'd never experienced before.

Chris let out a low groan of satisfaction, his eyes half lidded as he chewed. "You're gonna ruin me, you know that?"

Heat spread through me, pooling low in my belly. As much as I wanted to crawl under the table and go for round six—or was it seven?—this moment, us talking and getting to know each other, was just as good. Maybe better.

"It was my dad," I finally said, leaning back and resting my elbow on the table. "He was the one who got me into cooking."

Chris's gaze sharpened, curiosity sparking in his warm golden eyes. "Your dad?"

I nodded, a small smile tugging at my lips. "Yeah. He was a big fella—tough as they come—but he had this incredible passion for food. He used to say cooking wasn't just about feeding people; it was about telling a story, connecting with them."

Chris's lips quirked into a smile, and I could see him picturing it.

"He loved teaching me how to make the traditional stuff—damper, kangaroo stew, wattleseed pancakes. But he was also a master of fusion. He'd take bush tucker ingredients and mix them with techniques from all over the world. I used to watch him cook, and it was like watching a magician at work. Every meal was an experience, you know?"

Chris's smile grew wider. "So you inherited the magic."

I snorted, feeling heat creep up my neck. "I don't know about that, but yeah, I guess he passed it on. When I cook, it's like I'm carrying a piece of him with me."

He reached across the table and placed his large hand over mine, his touch grounding and reassuring. "Your dad sounds like an amazing man."

"He was," I said softly. "And he'd love this." I

gestured between us. "Sharing a meal, getting to know someone over food—that was his thing."

Chris's thumb traced a slow circle over my knuckles, his gaze locked on mine. "Then I owe him one for passing that on to you."

My chest tightened at his words, the sincerity in his tone. This man, who ate my food like it was his last meal on earth, who held my hand like it was something precious, was undoing me in ways I didn't even realise were possible.

"Careful," I said, my voice a little hoarse. "Keep talking like that, and I might have to cook for you every day."

His grin was wicked and utterly irresistible. "Promise?"

The laugh that bubbled out of me felt lighter than it had in years. Maybe, just maybe, I could get used to this. "We'll see. At the moment it's a tentative yes."

He quirked his brow at that but didn't push.

The truth was, we were in a bubble of chemistry and passion, and yesterday had pushed my limits, making me feel briefly untethered, not only with what went down but with what could have been.

What was it that Sandra Bullock said to the hot-as-sin Keanu Reeves? "Relationships that start under intense circumstances, they never last." I wanted to flip Sandy's character off that those words skipped around my brain. Hell, in *Speed 2*, Jack was nowhere to be seen.

"What's got you looking all tentative?" Chris's smile faded a little. "It's a look you usually wear when you're pissed off or overthinking."

My brows jumped high. "Is that right?"

"SICB agent, remember. I'm paid to know this shit."

I snorted when he grinned, my shoulders relaxing when he hooked his foot around my ankle. I contemplated coming up with some sort of bullshit, but yesterday we'd had bullets whizz by us, trying to take us out. I figured that meant we owed each other honesty or something. "I was thinking about that movie *Speed*."

Chris nodded. "I know the one." He eyed me, a picture of calm patience.

When I didn't say anything, sure if I did and shared the quote I'd sound like a dick, he reached out and smoothed his fingers over mine until I turned my hand palm up to hold his hand. My heart flipped at the gesture.

Chris's lips curved into a slow, knowing smile, the kind that made my stomach do strange flips.

"Let me guess. You're hung up on the part where Sandra Bullock says relationships that start under intense circumstances don't last?"

My mouth parted, but no sound came out. Damn it, he *did* know what I was thinking.

He chuckled, his thumb brushing over my knuckles. "You're forgetting something important about that quote."

"Oh, yeah?" I managed, my voice catching.

"Yeah." He leaned in just a little, close enough that his voice was a low rumble I could feel more than hear. "She said it. But she also kissed him at the end of the movie. That says something, don't you think?"

I blinked at him. "And what exactly does it say?"

"It says she was willing to take the risk. And if a movie star can risk it for a fictional cop who, let's be honest, probably wasn't half as charming as me, you can risk it for the real deal."

Fuck, he was smooth. I also didn't bother to challenge him that it was actually the character Annie, not the actress, who said those words.

There was no holding back my grin, not with so much cheesy perfection.

He parted his lips to speak but was cut off from my ringing mobile.

"Shit, I better get that. It's probably Yayi checking I'm alive and kicking as I didn't turn up on her doorstep this morning for a visit." I stood, feeling guilty that I hadn't even thought to call her. It went to show how blissfully distracting a big dick and multiple orgasms could be.

I frowned when I picked up my phone and read the name on the caller display. "Hello," I answered, my gut already dropping. The security firm hired to alert me about my restaurant's alarm going off could never be a good thing.

"Mr Munro, it's Alfie from SecureSite Alarms. We've received an alert from Kurranba. The alarm indicated a window was tampered with. We're sending a SecureSite unit around now to check. Can you confirm you're not on site?"

"No. I'm at home." I cast a glance at Chris, who was out of his seat, his phone already to his ear. Undoubtedly he could hear both sides of the conversation.

"And should there be anyone else on the premises?"

I checked the time. It was late. Tan had gone in to finalise the stock take, but that was hours ago. They'd messaged me just as they left with a final question. And that was about three hours back. "No.

None of my staff are there. My manager was the last person on site."

"That was Tanya Rollerston, correct?" Only Tan and I had alarm access, and each number was unique.

"Tan," I corrected. "They go by they and them, but yes, that's their current legal name." I jerked my attention to Chris as he held my shoes out to me. I glanced down, seeing he'd already put on his black boots and had tugged on his black tee.

I focussed on putting my running shoes on while still listening to Alfie explaining the next steps. As soon as my feet were wedged in, I allowed Chris to pull me to my car and didn't hesitate to get into the passenger seat.

"…ETA eight minutes," Alfie explained. "Our concern is that the camera is down, but the alert signalling a fault or it being turned off didn't enter our system."

"Okay. Well, I'm en route now," I said breathily, my heartbeat accelerating. "I'm six minutes away," I said, feeling the need to be oddly specific.

"Four," Chris said at my side, accelerating with a heavy foot the moment my seatbelt was clicked in.

"We don't advise owners to be on the scene until we receive the—"

"I'm with my... an SICB agent," I rushed to say, keeping my eyes on the road ahead, ignoring the tendril of mortification over my hesitation. What even I was about to say was beyond me. It didn't stop me from hiding my wince.

On the line, Alfie hesitated. "Uhm... okay. I'll let Samantha, who's on her way to Kurranba, know to expect you and a SICB agent."

"Three SICB agents." Chris cut in. "Two more are on their way."

My brows shot high, heat swelling in my chest, completely flustered.

"O-kay," Alfie responded, apparently hearing Chris's deep voice down the line. "We'll be in touch if we discover any information between now and then. We'll start looking into the video feed and what went wrong."

I swallowed hard, nodding despite being on the phone. "I'd appreciate that. Thank you." I ended the call and gripped the "oh fuck" handle as Chris took a corner at a speed I didn't know my car was capable of.

"You good?" he asked, keeping his gaze on the road ahead. We were just a couple of blocks away.

"Yeah." I huffed out a breath, surprised I wasn't bullshitting. Why wouldn't I be okay when I apparently had a team of agents at my back? My lips twitched, despite my franticly beating pulse.

"What's that smile for?"

I angled his way, appreciating his strong cheekbones and the day-old scruff I'd been enjoying feeling between my legs and scraping across my cheek all day. "Just starting to think you may be on to something."

"Yeah? What exactly?"

"That a relationship away from work, even with all the high-octane bullshit, just might be the start of something incredible."

His brows shot high, and pink filled his cheeks. Huh. Looked like Mr. Kick-Arse Agent wasn't immune to being taken by surprise. And from his hard swallow and the way he darted his tongue over his bottom lip, I had zero doubt that he liked what I said.

He screeched to a halt outside of Kurranba, the speed we were going and the sound of brakes doing nothing to hide our presence. Apparently we weren't in stealth mode.

Chris turned quickly, face angling close to mine. "You stay here and keep safe." He pressed his lips to mine, barely a whisper of a kiss before he pulled back. "And you'll find that I'm absolutely fucking right." One more kiss and I was alone. He raced out of the car before I could respond, let alone catch my breath.

Holy fuck, why the hell was that so hot? Competence and badassery were one hell of an aphrodisiac. But first, I gripped my seatbelt and leaned forwards to peer out of the window as I waited while Chris did his thing.

# 7

CHRIS

THE SCENT OF BURNT EARTH AND INCENSE FILLED MY nostrils. It wasn't one I'd smelt before. I tapped my comms, grateful I hadn't returned home at all so I still had all of my tactical gear. "Copy, Kent. Over."

"Kent here. Over. A scan of the area doesn't show any movement. But there are three blind spots in the two-block radius of Kurranba. Over."

"Copy that. How far out are Shaw and Michaels? Over." Michaels had been my first call as soon as I'd overheard the first words of Waru's phone call. Michaels had already been with his boyfriend, Shaw, making the request quicker. He'd then reached out to Kent and Lucas.

"ETA three minutes. Looks like the security rep

for the alarm system is stuck in traffic. Figures since their reputation is for shit. Over."

The muscle in my jaw ticked. Thank fuck I'd been with Waru. If I hadn't been and he'd come himself, beating the response unit.... I cracked my neck, continuing to walk around the building, scenting and looking for signs of disturbance as I did so.

A glint of metal caught my attention in the window in the alleyway. "Found something. Over."

"Copy."

A closer look revealed the broken lock. The window wasn't smashed, and beyond the slightly crooked steel lock, everything looked intact. "Sign of breach in third right window in alleyway. Over."

"Michaels checking in. One minute out. Over."

I settled at the sound of Michaels's voice. With three of us on the scene, one of us could stay with—

A thud, a smash, a yell.

Waru.

*Fuck.*

I charged around the building, shouting into comms, "Eyes on Waru. Now."

"Fuck." Kent sounded pissed, but it was the screech of tyres as the car accelerated that shot fury through my veins. Taillights were already fifteen metres away, glass on the ground next to where Waru's car should be parked.

"Stay on him, Kent," I ordered, voice tight. "I'm going to shift." There was no way I could keep pace on two feet. Four paws and I could give the car a good run for its money.

I willed the shift to come. No slow, deliberate change this time—I needed speed and raw power. The sharp sting of pain ripped through me as my body contorted. Bones realigned with a grinding sound. Muscles stretched and swelled. Fur erupted across my skin like wildfire.

The last remnants of my tactical gear shredded and fell away, leaving me stripped of everything human—including the comms earpiece that had been my lifeline to the team.

I couldn't call out to Kent now. Couldn't coordinate. It was just me, my instincts, and the drive to get Waru back.

My hands became massive paws, claws sinking into the asphalt. My arms and legs thickened, the change barrelling through me faster than ever before. A low growl tore from my throat, and my senses exploded with clarity. The world tilted as I dropped to all fours, now towering in my lion form.

The scent of Waru still lingered faintly in the air,

tainted by fear and that burnt earth and incense I couldn't place. My nostrils flared as I inhaled deeply, locking onto the trail. My ears twitched, picking up the hum of the engine carrying him away.

Shit. No time to think.

I sprang forwards, muscles bunching and releasing in perfect coordination. The world blurred as I bolted towards the scent, my paws striking the pavement in a steady rhythm. I stuck to the shadows as best I could—a hard task when you're a lion the size of a small car—but I'd trained for this. Years of tactical manoeuvres came rushing back, overriding every primal urge to roar and charge blindly.

Up ahead, the taillights swerved into an alley. My breath hitched as I poured on more speed, adrenaline surging.

I crouched low, ears swivelling as I tuned into the hum of the car engine fading in the distance. The scent of burnt earth and incense still clung to the air, mixed with Waru's fear—a smell that cut through me like a blade.

Each step landed with a soft tap on the pavement, creating a steady cadence as I pressed on, eating the distance between me and the bastard who'd taken him.

The taillights swerved sharply, disappearing behind a cluster of dilapidated buildings. I slowed, ears twitching as I approached. The unmistakable scent of Waru and the... I scented the air... vampire filled my nostrils, leading me to a grimy workshop tucked at the end of a dark alley.

A growl rumbled in my chest as I crept closer, claws scraping against the ground. Waru's voice filtered through the night, muffled but frantic.

"Please! You've got the wrong person—I don't know you!"

The sound sent a surge of rage through me. My tail flicked, muscles coiling as I crouched at the edge of the alley.

Through the workshop's cracked windows, I caught glimpses of movement. A tall figure—the vampire—dragged Waru roughly towards a table, shoving him down into a chair. Waru fought back, his jaw set with defiance even as fear poured off him in waves.

I couldn't hear Kent or the others, but I didn't need them to tell me what to do. The lion in me demanded action.

The vampire turned, pulling out a blade that glinted under the harsh fluorescent lights. Waru flinched but didn't look away. My claws flexed, scraping the concrete surrounding the workshop as I fought the urge to roar and charge blindly.

I couldn't storm in like a reckless beast. I had to be smart. Silent.

The door stood ajar, the vampire's arrogance leaving him careless. My size meant brute force would work, but subtlety might buy me the few seconds I needed to take him down without putting Waru at risk.

I crept closer, each step precise, my paws silent against the ground. My heart thundered, every instinct screaming to protect the man I'd barely had time to know but already couldn't imagine losing.

The scent of Waru's fear sharpened, and my growl slipped free before I could stop it.

The vampire froze, head snapping towards the door. "What the hell was that?"

Dammit. So much for subtlety.

With a snarl, I surged forwards, hitting the steel door at full speed. It buckled inwards with a deafening crash, sending the vampire staggering back.

The room erupted into chaos.

Waru's eyes widened as he caught sight of me, his lips parting in shock. "Chris?"

The vampire recovered quickly, snarling as he drew the blade and lunged towards me.

Big mistake.

I roared, the sound shaking the walls, and launched myself at him. My claws found flesh, raking across his chest as my massive body slammed into him. The blade clattered to the ground as he crumpled under my weight.

But I didn't stop there. Not until I was sure he wasn't getting back up.

Waru's voice broke through the haze of fury, trembling but strong. "Chris, stop! You've got him!"

I turned, panting, my massive frame heaving with adrenaline. Waru stood frozen, his eyes locked on me, wide but full of something I couldn't quite place.

Relief. Or I hoped like hell that was what it was.

I stepped closer, lowering my head as my tail flicked behind me. Waru reached out hesitantly, his hand trembling as it brushed against my mane.

"Holy shit," he whispered, his voice cracking. "You came for me."

His touch grounded me, pulling me back from the brink. My instincts wanted to keep going, to rip and tear until the threat was nothing but shreds— but Waru's hand on my fur reminded me why I was here.

I huffed softly, nudging his chest with my nose.

He exhaled shakily, his fingers curling into my mane.

"Thank you," he murmured.

I rumbled in response, my gaze flicking towards the crumpled vampire on the floor. He wasn't dead—not yet, and unfortunately not ever. The need to follow the law stilled my hand. But taking him into custody to discover why he'd gone after Waru in the first place was my priority.

The sound of Michaels's car engine cut through the air. I exhaled. They'd take care of the vampire. I suspected we had another sixty seconds until he was conscious. All that mattered was getting Waru out of here.

Safe.

---

"What do you mean it's unrelated?" Confusion rippled through me. I didn't believe in coincidences, especially ones that smelt like bullshit.

"I don't buy it." Michaels shook his head.

Frustration slammed into me. "But you just said—"

"I recounted what the vampire said and am reiterating that, for whatever fucked reason or hardcore history said vampire has, he's not breaking."

Jaw clenching, I stared through the two-way mirror at the smug-looking vampire. He'd fully healed, but his shirt was ripped, and blood covered his face and chest. It didn't give me any satisfaction.

Turner, the vampire, a name that checked out in the system, had no priors. He also lived within five blocks of Waru's restaurant. His story, which he appeared determined to stick to, was he was a stalker, infatuated by Waru and his killer cooking skills.

The whole thing was ludicrous. Not that Waru wasn't hot or skilled enough to warrant catching a stalker's attention, which sounded all levels of dodgy that I even thought that, but still, Turner was a lying liar who lied. And that right there—my eloquence—pretty much summed up how fucking pissed off I was.

Waru had been shaken up but remained remarkably together. He'd let Michaels interview him as I sat by his side, holding his hand. Thankfully Michaels had shown a rare moment of keeping his mouth shut and hadn't commented on the way I clung to Waru, because I was absolutely the man who hadn't wanted to let him go, let alone have him out of my sight.

The latter was probably why tension vibrated through my limbs. Shaw had taken Waru to get a hot chocolate, while I was left here thinking about everything Waru had told us had been said. Which had been jack shit. Beyond Turner smashing the window and giving him one hard punch that still made me clench my teeth, the vampire hadn't said anything beyond professing his adoration of Waru's lemon myrtle cheesecake.

And the knife...? Turner had wanted to eat said cheesecake from Waru's naked body. Like, what the fuck? Who even ate cheesecake with a damn knife? Why not a spoon or a fork? It all added up to just how full of shit he was.

Fuck. Just the thought had me grinding my teeth and considering if Michaels would look the other way if spent some time alone with Turner in the interrogation room.

"Shit."

I snapped my attention to Michaels, wondering why he was cussing. "What is it? What's wrong?"

He rubbed the back of his neck, seeming to struggle to settle on an emotion. "I think we're going to have to call Callen."

Understanding slammed into me. I'd heard the stories, but I had no clue how true they were. "You think that'll work? You think he can make Turner break?"

Michaels shrugged, even as he pulled out his phone. "I don't know, man. The last time he worked his magic in the interrogation room, he got the answers no one else could. He wouldn't let anyone but Thatch watch, and there were no recordings."

My brows shot high. Thatch was the head of the ITU before he moved to join the SICB Academy, where he'd since been promoted to chief instructor. He was also Callen's saner half and had used to be his boss. He was also a stickler for rules and following protocol. Unlike the division leader, who seemed to make a game out of breaking rules and seeing how far he could push Director Durrant, leader of the SICB.

I didn't have the chance to respond before he was talking to Callen, explaining the situation, and asking for his special skill set.

Colour me curious, but I hoped to get to watch him in action to see what all the fuss was about. More than that, though, I really hoped he had some special mojo up his sleeves. We needed to figure out if Waru was at risk.

I spent time with Waru before Callen arrived. The trembling in his hands had stopped, and the bruise on his jaw had almost faded.

"I can organise for you to go home, have someone watch the house." The first time I'd offered, he'd shot me down. I was grateful for it, not wanting him far away. But exhaustion bit at his heels, making his usually rich brown skin look dull.

"No." Creases formed between his brows. "Unless you want me to leave."

"No," I answered quickly. "That's the last thing I want."

His brow smoothed out. "Yeah?"

I squeezed his hand. "Definitely. We might be in for a wait, or it might just be another hour. I've no idea yet." We'd brought both Waru and Turner to an on-the-books SICB location that had no association with the ITU. It made life tricky at times, working as a covert unit. We weren't quite off the books, but we were as close as you could get to being ghosts.

The whole team had official SICB identities in bogus and innocuous divisions. We also each carried several aliases. It was no wonder that ITU relation-ships bordered on incestuous, which honestly, I'd taken delight a time or twelve saying to the members of the team who dated in-house.

To tell Waru the truth, I'd need to get approval from not only Lucas as team leader and Callen but also Director Durrant. If Waru and I reached that point, though, it would be worth weaving through the red tape so I could be completely honest with him.

Or as honest as any agent could be who worked with top secret cases for the bureau.

"I can wait." A soft, tired smile appeared before he leaned against me, taking comfort. I swallowed hard, not used to being in this situation. Not used to offering even a semblance of softness. It was a feeling I could get addicted to. Or maybe it was Waru who'd be the object of my fixation.

*Stalker my arse.* The thought hit me, and I released a snort, earning me raised brows from Waru.

"Copy, Chris. You might want to peel yourself away from your chef. Callen's in the lift."

The lift dinged, and I glanced towards the door. Callen strode out first, exuding the confidence of a man who was in charge—technically. It still threw the team off sometimes, seeing him as the division leader. Not because he wasn't incredible at the job, but because he took such obvious joy in breaking every rule and shredding red tape into confetti.

Behind him, Kent followed, her expression hovering between exasperation and amusement, her usual state when dealing with Callen.

"Fancy seeing you here, boss," I said, unable to keep the wryness out of my tone. "Figured you'd still be arguing with Durrant about that whole 'protocols are optional' thing."

Callen smirked, the picture of unbothered authority. "Turns out the director loves me. Probably because I save her ass on a regular basis."

Kent snorted, dropping into her chair at her workstation. "Or because you're too much trouble to fire. Like a feral cat that keeps showing up no matter how many times you lock the door."

"Thanks for the support, Kent," Callen deadpanned. "Remind me to dock your snacks budget later."

"As if you could function without me." She tapped a few keys when she reached the bank of monitors to the left of the room, pulling up the surveillance feeds with her usual efficiency. "Anyway, enough about your dubious leadership style. Chris, I've got the traffic cams. Caught the tail end of your liony joyride and tracked the car to the mechanics. You're welcome."

I rolled my eyes. "Appreciate it, Kent."

She turned in her chair, raising an eyebrow. "That it? No grovelling? No declaration of my unmatched brilliance?"

"Appreciate it, Kent," I repeated. "You're terrifyingly competent and mildly scary, as always."

She smirked, swivelling back towards the monitors. "Acceptable. I'll let it slide this time."

Callen leaned against the desk, arms crossed, his grin as wide as ever. "Still letting her bully you, huh? I thought you were supposed to be the one running this one."

"As if Kent doesn't pull every string in the ITU," I shot back, gesturing to the screen. "Unlike you, she doesn't need to play to the crowd to be useful." My lips twisted into a smirk, so grateful I had a boss, or technically my boss's boss, who played like one of the team.

Callen clutched his chest in mock outrage. "I provide morale, thank you very much. The glue that holds this whole circus together. And I'm absolutely telling Lucas you said Kent's the not-so-secret boss around here."

Kent raised an eyebrow, still tapping away at her

keyboard. "You're more like the glitter that gets everywhere and doesn't wash out. Annoying, but we've learned to live with it."

"Harsh but fair," Callen conceded, turning to Waru. "And you must be the chef. Heard a lot about you. Mostly that you've managed to put up with Chris longer than most people can handle."

Waru blinked, glancing between us. "Uh, yeah. Waru."

"Welcome to the chaos." Callen's grin turned mischievous. "Don't let Kent scare you. She only bites if you touch her snacks."

"That's not true," Kent said without looking up. "I bite if you touch my snacks, my gear, or my chair."

"Duly noted," Waru said, his lips twitching like he was trying not to laugh.

Callen glanced at me, his expression briefly softening before he slipped back into leader mode. "What's our next move?"

"Kent's already on it," I said, deferring to her expertise.

"Already on it, and I dug so deep that I hit secrets so buried, they probably had their own postcode. Workshop's flagged as a Kole asset." Her words were so nonchalant, I almost missed them.

"For real?"

She shot me a deadpan look, not even bothering to arch a brow at me.

"Fair," I mumbled, shifting a little uncomfortably as Waru's gaze ping-ponged between the three of us. In all honesty, I half expected Callen to ask Waru to leave, not that I was going to draw his attention to the fact I still sat here, clutching my panther's hand.

"Good. Anything actionable yet, Kent?"

She swivelled back to the monitors, pulling up a blueprint of the workshop on the main screen. "I've mapped potential weak points for entry, in case Chris wants to play King of the Jungle again. Just tell me you're not planning to shred another set of gear. I'm not the quartermaster."

"Noted," I said, ignoring Callen's amused snort.

"I think the workshop is a dead end, though. All it's confirmed is a connection between stalkerboy and Kole. What we need to know is why he infiltrated Waru's restaurant and why he took off with Waru when Chris arrived at the scene."

"Perfect," Callen said, his tone light but his gaze sharp as a blade. He clapped his hands once. "Kent, keep eyes on the feeds. Chris, stick with Waru and stay alert. I'll take the lead in the interrogation."

Waru's eyes darted between us, his brow

furrowed, clearly trying to make sense of the whirl-wind of activity and Callen's almost-casual confidence.

"Relax, chef," Callen said with a crooked grin. "This is how we get things done—looks like chaos, but it works. Promise."

"Looks like chaos because it *is* chaos," Kent muttered, never glancing away from her screens. "And it works because I'm here to stop it from imploding."

Callen gave a mock-offended scoff, but his grin only widened. "What can I say? I thrive under pressure." He turned to me. "And apparently, my ability to sweet-talk answers out of people has earned me the job tonight. You'll see why. Or maybe you won't, since most of it's classified."

Waru blinked, and I had to bite back a smirk at the mix of curiosity and exasperation on his face. Callen thrived on this energy—the confidence, the mystery, the control. It was why he had the job despite his tendency to colour outside the lines.

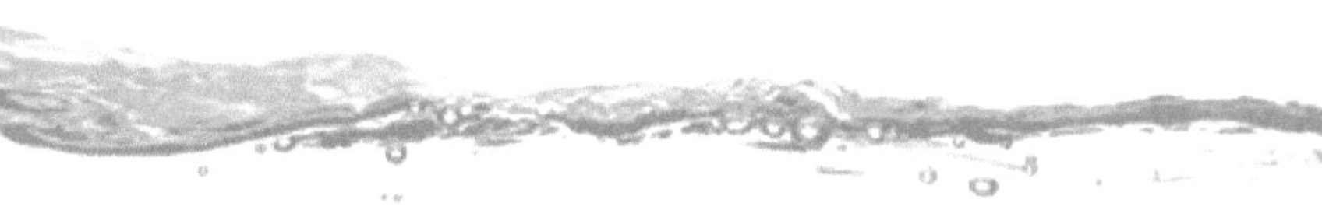

# 8

WARU

My gut hollowed out as I edged further into Kurranba.

By some miracle, there wasn't anything out of place. No bullet holes decorated the walls, and the furniture wasn't smashed to smithereens. Beyond the broken latch on the one window, everything looked exactly as it should: set up for the following day's opening. I suspected Tan had something to do with how immaculate the place was since we'd been ushered out mid-service just yesterday.

Fuck, was that really just yesterday? So much had happened in such a short space of time, it was no wonder I struggled to process.

But all those thoughts did was offer me the tiniest distraction from the real reason I was surrounded by SICB agents while stepping into the restaurant I'd purchased just seven years ago.

I just hadn't realised at the time I'd purchased it from Brax's uncle.

"Over here." I attempted to step away from Chris, only for him to clamp his hand on my waist, tugging me to his side.

"Where? You tell us, and Michaels and Shaw will check it out."

I worked hard not to sigh into Chris, unused to feeling taken care of. It was a heady feeling being doted on like this. Protected. I was so used to calling the shots in the kitchen and running every single minute I was in the restaurant with well-oiled precision, to hand the reins over was different. Liberating.

Something I could get used to.

"Yeah, okay." I pointed to the small cupboard door not visible from where we stood. "Below the counter is a small hatch. You need to push against it, and it'll pop open. There you'll find the key."

Michaels moved to gather the key, holding it out when he'd found it. "This it?"

"Yeah." I indicated towards the small corridor. "In my office, you'll find a bookcase. There's a button underneath the third shelf on the right. It'll unlatch the bookcase and reveal the door."

Chris didn't let go of me, his arm firm yet careful around my waist as if he knew I might bolt. It wasn't fear that made my legs feel unsteady—it was something heavier, more unsettling. Betrayal, maybe. By a building. A place I'd poured so much of myself into, only to learn it had harboured secrets that could've gotten me killed.

I forced myself to stay still, watching Michaels and Shaw move towards the office with quick, deliberate steps. The ease with which they worked together, the unspoken coordination, reminded me that they weren't just any security team—they were professionals in a league far beyond anything I'd ever seen.

Not that I had much to go on beyond what I'd seen in the movies.

"Hey." Chris's voice broke through my haze. "You okay?"

I shook my head, not trusting myself to speak for a moment. Then I gestured around the space I'd worked so hard to make my own. "I bought this place because it felt right. Like I could turn it into something amazing. And now... now I find out it was just a dumping ground for Brax's mess."

Chris frowned, his golden eyes sharp and unwavering. "None of this is on you. You didn't know."

While true, I struggled to not feel responsible. If only I'd investigated the creepy basement. When I'd discovered the secret door, I'd been beyond excited. But after ten minutes too long down there—in a basement with no electricity and the scent of cold stone preventing me from smelling the earth—I'd hightailed it out of there. It made sense I hated the feel of the place since it was used by Brax to stash evidence against Kole that could get him killed or help him take over her business.

Shaw's voice cut through my overloaded brain. "Got it," he said, emerging from the office. He held up a heavy, leatherbound ledger—the kind that seemed to carry the weight of a thousand secrets.

"This it?" Michaels asked, gesturing to the book.

Chris nodded grimly. "That's got to be it."

"Lots of names in here," Shaw added. "Dates. Transactions. Looks like Kole's personal blackmail file."

The air left my lungs in a rush. That unassuming book had nearly cost me my life.

"I still can't believe it was Brax's uncle who sold me this place," I said, the words tumbling out as if speaking them would make them easier to bear.

"Back then, I thought I'd lucked out. I didn't know the guy. Never met him in person—everything went through the real estate agent. But I'd never met Brax nor heard of him. Why would I?" I swallowed hard, forcing myself to continue, "Brax must've thought he was being clever, using this place to stash the ledger. He probably figured his uncle's place would be the last place Kole would look. Do you think she knew he had it all along?"

Chris exhaled slowly, his hand rubbing soothing circles against my back.

Michaels answered, "From what we know about Kole, very little gets past her."

"I mean, it worked... for a while," I said bitterly. "Until it didn't. Kole found out about the ledger and about Brax's side hustle. It's why he was nearly killed, isn't it?"

Chris nodded. "She doesn't leave loose ends. That he survived at all is a miracle."

"And now I'm the loose end."

"You're not," Chris said firmly, his voice cutting through the despair threatening to pull me under. "We've got the ledger now. Kole can't use it against you—or anyone else."

"Good." I took a shaky breath. "Take it. I don't want it anywhere near this place."

Shaw nodded. "We'll secure it."

As the team moved with purpose, I glanced around Kurranba again. It was my sanctuary, my dream made real. And now, it felt like a stranger to me.

Chris pulled me closer, his voice soft but steady. "You're still standing. That's what matters."

I looked up at him, my chest tightening at the sincerity in his eyes. "Barely."

"Barely counts." He smiled—a real smile this time—and it was enough to chase away some of the bitterness clinging to me. "You're tenacious, remember? You're not going to let some shady basement and a vampire ruin your dream."

The warmth spread, chasing away some of the bitterness. "You think so?"

"I know so." He nudged me gently, his expression softening in a way that made my heart do a strange little flip. "Come on. Let's get you out of here. You can figure out what's next when you're not in the middle of all this."

I hesitated, my gaze lingering on the polished floors and neatly set tables. Tan had done their job well.

And so would I.

"Okay," I said finally, leaning into Chris as we turned to leave. "Let's go."

---

I KNEADED CHRIS'S BUTT-CHEEKS, MY GRIN QUICK TO come when he released a loud groan that sounded like sin. After stopping by Chris's apartment for him to collect a change of clothes, we'd then headed back to my house.

We'd eaten, made out on the sofa, then scrubbed each other down with exploring fingers and mouths, which led us to now. Shifting could be brutal for some species—for panthers, not so much. Regardless, it was as necessary as breathing.

But with the speed Chris had shifted when coming to my rescue, no doubt it left a residual ache behind that he'd likely feel for a few hours yet. A transformation like that left its mark. The same would have happened to me had I even attempted a shift that fast.

Working my fingers over Chris's muscles was the price I willingly paid for all he'd done.

"Are you trying to ruin me?" Each breathy sigh that escaped Chris rolled over me like a heady caress. I loved I could make him melt, unravel him so it felt like his aching bones turned to jelly.

"Maybe." I pressed a kiss to the back of his neck, continuing to work the warm oil into his skin.

Chris made it impossibly easy to let my guard down. A skill I didn't think I should make him aware of. Christ knew what else he could make me do. Eat Macca's.... I barely suppressed a shudder. Fuck, I wondered if he could talk me into—

"Did you just say you wanted to eat Macca's?"

I blanched. The man was so dangerous that I didn't realise I was mumbling away aloud.

"Eat Macca's... I think not." Not that eating a McDonald's a time or twelve in my youth hadn't gotten me out of a tough spot. A secret I'd take with me to my grave.

Chris turned his head just enough to smirk at me, his expression equal parts smug and devastatingly charming. "Don't act like it's beneath you. Fries are universal."

"Universal garbage," I shot back, ignoring the thought of how satisfying eating grease-infused fries could be. Instead, I focussed on kneading my thumbs into the tense line of his shoulders.

He groaned, the sound sinful enough to make

me pause. "Keep doing that, and I bet I could get you to eat a Filet-O-Fish."

I snorted, leaning closer so my lips brushed his ear. "Don't push your luck. You're not *that* charming."

Chris hummed, entirely too pleased with himself. "Give me time, chef. Everyone's got a breaking point."

"Mine's food poisoning," I deadpanned.

"Yet here you are," he murmured, letting his head fall forwards under my touch. "Falling under my spell. One fry at a time."

"Dream on," I muttered, but the warmth in my chest betrayed the smile tugging at my lips.

Without warning, he turned, almost bucking me off from where I sat astride his thighs before he caught hold of my waist to stop me from falling. Once on his back, he settled me on the top of his thighs, our cocks brushing. Matching moans spilled free as I tried and failed to tear my eyes away from his cock.

"It should be illegal to have such a pretty dick." My tone was all matter of fact.

Chris snorted out a laugh. "Is that right?"

"Yup." A smirk curved my lips. "How are your muscles feeling?"

The pads of his fingers rubbed in gentle circles across my skin. "So much better. Thank you."

"So, you're relaxed and unwound enough to sleep?" The arch of my brow made my intentions pretty damn clear that energy still buzzed through body. I was more than okay for him to harness it.

Chris darted his gaze around my face, not letting up his slow, sensual circles. "I've still got muscles you haven't touched tonight, if you're interested."

Subtlety went flying out of the window when my dick jerked. "Is that right? That not too strenuous for you tonight?" While I desperately, eagerly wanted to be balls deep inside him, we were both bordering on exhaustion slamming into us.

"If you're happy to stay almost right where you are, then I think I can manage just fine." His tone screamed sex and promise and the possibility of a tomorrow. And how he managed all of that in a few simple words was beyond me, but I wanted it all.

More than anything, I wanted to fuck him into the mattress. My cock wept at the possibility, a bead of precum dripping to the underside of my cock and landing on his balls.

A shuddery breath escaped Chris, his eyes flaring with heat when I moved to settle between his legs after I took hold of the bottle of lube we'd left next to us on the mattress.

"I've got a feeling this is going to go fast."

Satisfaction filled his expression. "Even after coming three times already?"

"With my cock deep inside you—" I didn't hold back the shudder rippling over me as I gripped the base of my cock. "—fuck, I'll be lucky to get two long strokes in before I fill you with my cum."

"Fuck...." The word tore free from Chris with a moan. "That's okay. Just get inside me. There's always tomorrow."

I slowed my fingers as I worked them inside his tight channel. "Is that, right?" I pushed deeper, and Chris parted his knees wider.

"Uh-huh."

"And what if I only last three strokes?" I slipped my two fingers out before breaching him with three.

"*Nngh.*" He exhaled and swiped his tongue over his bottom lip, leaving it shiny and just begging to be kissed.

"What then?" I pushed, a glutton for punishment, and apparently needy as fuck and wanting to know if he was on the same page I was.

"Then," he all but whimpered, "we go again the

next day, and the next, and every single fucking day of the week, the month, the year."

"Fuck." I couldn't resist any longer, I slammed my mouth to his, drinking in his groans, sliding my tongue against him, wanting his words to be our reality.

But we could make it work and figure this out.

"Okay," I mumbled breathily before coming up for air and pressing my cock against his slick entrance. "Now *that* we can do." I slid home, pausing for a second to commit the moment to memory.

As far as I was concerned, *Speed 2* should never have happened. Annie and Jack totally had the chemistry that could last a lifetime. As I eased out before pistoning my hips and pulling every delicious moan from Chris that I could, I just knew he was worth the risk.

# ACKNOWLEDGMENTS

I'm so thankful so many of you asked for Chris's story. He absolutely deserves his HEA. So, my readers, thank you for encouraging me with this series. A giant, special thank-you for purchasing this limited-edition set.

A huge shout out to my wonderful team who support me from concept to publication—Chelsea, Claire at BookSmith Designs, and my team of Hot Tree Editing editors and support staff. I couldn't do any of this without such wonderful support.

A special thanks to my family who support me through the mayhem.

# About the Author

Becca Seymour is a British/Aussie author and the #1 gay romance best seller of the True-Blue series. Known for "steamy and endearing" and "emotionally profound love stories" (InD'tale Magazine) her books have been nominated for multiple RONE Awards.

Becca has a sweet tooth for marshmallow-hearted monsters, swoon-worthy supernatural studs, and everyday guys and basketball players with hearts of gold. If you like your MM romance sweet, spicy, and occasionally action-packed, slip into stalker mode and fall hard for her True-Blue and Minnesota Eagles men—and maybe a shifter or monster two.

To check for updates head to my website:

https://beccaseymour.com

https://landing.mailerlite.com/webforms/landing/

r9f0i4

Plus, join my Facebook group:

HTTPS://WWW.FACEBOOK.COM/GROUPS/ROMMANCEWITH BECCALOUISA/

JOIN ME ON PATREON FOR EARLY CHAPTERS, SPECIAL EDITION BOOKS, REVEALS, & MORE: PATREON.COM/ BECCASEYMOUR

facebook.com/beccaseymourauthor

instagram.com/authorbeccaseymour

bookbub.com/authors/becca-seymour

tiktok.com/@beccaseymourwrites